# SURVIVOR
## TITANIC

For Emily, Sam, Edward and Alexander.

While this book is based on real characters and actual historical events,
some situations and people are fictional, created by the author.

Scholastic Children's Books,
Euston House, 24 Eversholt Street,
London NW1 1DB, UK

A division of Scholastic Ltd
London ~ New York ~ Toronto ~ Sydney ~ Auckland
Mexico City ~ New Delhi ~ Hong Kong

First published in the UK by Scholastic Ltd, 2017

ISBN 978 1407 17875 2

Printed and bound by
CPI Group (UK) Ltd, Croydon, CR0 4YY

2 4 6 8 10 9 7 5 3 1

Papers used by Scholastic Children's Books
are made from woods grown in sustainable forests.

www.scholastic.co.uk

STEPHEN DAVIES

# SURVIVOR
## TITANIC

SCHOLASTIC

# CHAPTER

"Hey Ralph, can we swap bunks tonight?"

"Why?" My older brother sounded suspicious. "You gonna be kicking my bed springs, Jimmy? Is that it?"

"'Course not, Ralph," I said, trying to sound all innocent. "I just want to try the bottom bunk."

"Fine. But no monkeying around, do you hear me?"

Mam switched out the lights and lay down in her bed next to our bunk bed.

"Sweet dreams, boys," she said. "Only three sleeps

till we reach New York. Three sleeps until we see your pa again and start our new life in America."

The massive engines of the *Titanic* thumped and growled beneath us, and the steady heaving of the ship rocked us to sleep.

At least, it rocked Mam and Ralph. Me, I pinched myself to stay awake. My plans for the night did not include falling asleep.

As soon as it was safe, I slid out of bed and arranged a fake 'Jimmy' under the blankets. I rolled-up clothes for the body and used Ralph's football for the head. Then I crept across the cabin and slipped out, closing the cabin door as quietly as I could.

I climbed the stairs, laughing to myself at the thought of the decoy in my bed and excited by the adventure ahead of me. I had heard stories of the wild parties in the third-class common room at the front of the ship, and now I was going to see one for myself.

The port-side corridor on E deck was the longest corridor in the whole ship. The crew nicknamed it Scotland Road. As I ran along it, the sound of music and laughter grew louder, and when I climbed the last staircase I found myself in the middle of the best party I had ever seen.

A banjo player and an accordion player stood on a table in the middle of the room, playing their instruments hard and fast. The floor around them was filled with men and women clapping and stomping so hard that the whole room shook. I recognized the tune as 'The Little Beggarman', one of the folk songs Pa used to sing when we all lived together back in Kilkenny, before Pa left for America.

*I am a little beggarman and begging I have been*
*For three score years in this little isle of green.*

Some of the men and women in the crowd formed lines and began dancing just like they did back home in Ireland. They kept their bodies still but their legs moved like crazy – skipping, kicking and hopping to the music. The rest of the crowd threw back their heads and sang their hearts out. I reckon even the people of New York, tucked up in their beds four thousand miles away, must have heard 'The Little Beggarman' that night.

A dark-eyed man in a smart suit joined the musicians on top of the table. He held a pear-shaped instrument I hadn't seen before and began plucking its strings with something that looked like a feather.

> *I slept in the barn down at Caurabawn,*
> *The night was wet and I slept till dawn,*
> *With holes in the roof and the rain*
>     *coming through*
> *And the rats and the cats, they were playing*
>     *peek-a-boo!*

Just as we sang the rats-and-cats bit, a real live rat streaked under the table and dashed among the dancers. People screamed and pointed. Some jumped onto chairs and tables and others rushed after the rat, laughing their heads off.

"Somebody catch it!" they cried.

I ducked and dodged through the crowd, closing in on the rat. I've caught a few rodents in my time and the secret is simple – don't try to chase it, head it off. And don't grab where it is, grab where it's *going* to be.

I dived to the floor and cupped my hands in front of the scurrying rat.

"*Gotcha!*" I cried, but I had spoken too soon. Another hand shot out in front of mine to grab the rat. Our heads banged together hard and I blacked out.

# CHAPTER

When I came to, I saw that the head and hand belonged to another boy about my age. The boy was now jumping around like a mad thing, waving the rat triumphantly in the air. Everyone cheered and the accordion piped up again.

The boy knelt down beside me. He had dark eyes and thick curly hair.

"Bad luck," he said.

I rubbed my head. The room around me still seemed to be spinning.

"Bad luck, my foot," I snapped. "You should watch where you're going, you plonker."

The boy frowned. "What's a plonker?"

"A clumsy person," I replied.

The boy swapped the rat into his left hand and stuck out his right hand for me to shake. "I'm Omar," he said.

"I'm Jimmy," I said. "Where are you from?"

"Lebanon," said Omar. "But my dad taught me English when I was very young. He says you need English if you want to travel the world. That's him, up on the table there. The one with the oud."

"The what?"

"The oud. It's the name of that string instrument he's playing. The one shaped like a teardrop.'

I looked at the oud player, who was now surrounded by dark-haired men and women. These men and women were doing a dance that looked surprisingly similar to our Irish line dancing, only with longer steps.

Omar started to do the dance, loping first one way and then the other.

"It's a Lebanese dance," he shouted above the music. "We call it roof dancing."

"Roof dancing!" I could not help laughing at that.

"Houses back home in Lebanon have flat roofs made of mud," said Omar. "Every year we put new mud on the roof and invite all our friends to come and dance on it. A roof dance packs the mud tight and stops the roof from leaking."

I stood up and tried a few steps of the roof dance, but I soon tripped over my feet and tumbled to the floor again.

Omar doubled up with laughter. "Now who's a plonker?"

We wandered over to one of the food tables and ate some apple slices and crackers. Omar gave a bit of cracker to the rat, who nibbled it eagerly.

"So, Jimmy," Omar said. "What do you think of the *Titanic*?"

"Grand," I replied. "I've spent hours exploring it."

"Me too." Omar's eyes shone. "If there's anything worth knowing about this ship, I know it."

"Bet you don't know the name of the captain."

"Captain Edward Smith," said Omar proudly.

"I bet you don't know where the ice-cream kitchen is."

"I do," said Omar. "I've been inside it – and I've been chased out, too!"

"What about the squash court?"

"Seen it."

"Mail room? Barber shop? Dog kennels?"

"Seen all of those," said Omar. "What about you? Have you been to the cargo holds, where they keep the luggage?"

"I went to hold number four," I said. "I saw a big crate marked 'marmalade machine'."

"You should have tried hold number two," said Omar. "There are some crates marked 'dragon's blood'."

"What?" I stared at him. "You're joking, right?"

"No joke," said Omar. "I'll show you in the morning, if you like."

# CHAPTER

# 3

Growing up in Kilkenny, Ralph and I always had porridge for breakfast. On the *Titanic* we could have porridge if we wanted it, but we could also have jacket potatoes, smoked herrings, beef steak and as much fresh bread and marmalade as we could eat.

As I climbed the steps into the third-class dining room, I saw Omar already standing at a food table, piling his plate high with steak and onions. I ran up behind him and pinched the back of his neck.

"Hey!" Omar squealed. "You nearly made me drop my plate."

"It's going to break anyway if you put any more of that steak on it," I said.

Omar laughed. "I'm telling you, Jimmy, if this is a third-class breakfast, I'm happy to stay third class for the rest of my life!"

As we ate our breakfast, Omar told me about his family. He was travelling with his parents, his two older sisters and his four-year-old brother, Tannus. His dad was a famous musician in Lebanon and was hoping to make his fortune in America. Their journey so far had been long and difficult. In the last three weeks Omar had ridden on a donkey, two boats and two trains.

"What an adventure!" I said. "You must be pretty tired."

"Not any more," he replied. "You can't be tired on the *Titanic*. It's too exciting."

"That reminds me. When are you going to show me the dragon's blood?"

Omar stood up and put his last piece of steak in his pocket. "Right now."

He led the way up the staircase and forward

along Scotland Road. But instead of going up to the common room, we went down two flights of steps into the belly of the ship.

"You've taken a wrong turn," I said. "There's nothing here but third-class cabins."

"Trust me," said Omar.

He stopped outside cabin 248, pressed his ear to the door, then turned the handle and went in. The cabin was bigger than ours, with three bunk beds and lots of luggage.

"Whose cabin is this?" I asked.

"Mine," said Omar. "Don't worry, my family are up in the dining room eating their breakfast."

"I thought we were going to a cargo hold."

"We are."

Omar took a coin from his pocket and crawled under one of the bunk beds. "There's an air vent here," he said. "If I unscrew the front bit, we can just about get through."

I knelt down. When my eyes got used to the darkness underneath the bed, I saw a metal plate lying flat and Omar's feet disappearing through a narrow vent.

# CHAPTER

"Your turn." Omar's voice sounded muffled and far away. "Be careful, though. There's quite a long drop on this side."

"You're even crazier than I am," I muttered, crawling under the bed.

I wriggled through the narrow gap and found myself staring down into a large, dimly lit luggage hold piled high with crates. Omar swung hand over hand along a thick metal pipe and dropped down onto a pile of mattresses. I followed suit and landed next to him, bouncing high on the brand new mattress springs.

Omar got to his feet, bent his knees and did two quick backflips.

"Dragon's blood?" I reminded him.

"Oh yes." Omar climbed down off the mattresses, made his way over to a stack of crates on the starboard side. "There," he said, pointing.

## DRAGON'S BLOOD:
## HANDLE WITH CARE

I had to read it twice because I didn't believe my eyes at first. "Incredible!" I gasped.

"Keep your voice down," Omar whispered. "Someone will hear us."

I approached the stack of crates and ran my hand across them. They were made of dark wooden slats and covered in a thin layer of dust. I reached up and felt along the top crate until my hands found wooden handles on either side.

"What are you doing?" said Omar.

"I'm going to look inside."

Omar stared at me. "You can't do that!"

"Why not?"

"It's probably magic or something."

"Magic? Don't be daft," I told him. I dragged the top crate towards me so that its weight was on my chest, then lowered it gently to the floor. A beetle scuttled across my hand and disappeared into the shadows.

"I'm not being daft!" said Omar. "If it's not dangerous, why does it say 'handle with care'?"

"All the crates say handle with care!" I took my penknife out of my pocket. "I'm opening it, Omar, and you can't stop me."

I wedged the blade under the corner of the lid and prised it upwards. A sweet, spicy smell filled my nostrils.

Omar grabbed my arm. "Jimmy, please!" His face was white with fear.

"Calm down, Omar!" I squeezed my fingers into the gap and started to pull the lid open inch by inch. The wooden slats creaked eerily.

"Here it comes," I whispered. "Any second now—"

"Oi!" cried a voice.

The voice was not Omar's.

I looked up sharply and saw a barrel-chested man in a dark blue uniform. He was about twelve paces away from us and the surprise in his eyes had already turned to anger. I stood up and backed away slowly.

"Oi!" the sailor yelled again. "What are you two boys doing with that crate?"

"Nothing," I croaked.

"You're trying to open it, you thieving little poxbottles." He advanced towards us with open arms, like a farmer trying to catch a hen.

"Jimmy," Omar whispered. "I think we should probably run."

# CHAPTER

# 5

The sailor lunged forward and made a grab for us, but we were too nimble for him. We dodged backwards out of his reach, darted behind the stack of dragon's blood and sprinted along a narrow alleyway between two rows of luggage crates.

"Come here, you little tykes!" roared the sailor. "I should throw you overboard!"

The alleyway led out into an open space. Raised up on wooden blocks, was a Renault towncar, the finest motor car I had ever seen. Even in the dim light of the cargo hold, its burgundy body and brass fittings gleamed.

We hid behind the Renault, not daring to take a breath. Peering through its windows, we could see the sailor prowling around the hold, listening for the slightest sound.

"That door behind him," Omar whispered in my ear. "I don't think it's shut properly. I'll create a diversion and then we'll make a run for it."

I nodded.

Omar took a marble from his pocket and threw it gently behind a stack of crates. It clattered and rolled.

The sailor ran towards the noise, and we rushed for the door.

On the other side of the door was a spiral staircase. We sprinted up it, taking the steps three at a time. The sailor stormed up the steps behind us in furious pursuit.

"I've never been here," I gasped. "Where are we?"

"Crew's staircase at the front of the ship."

"Bow, not front," I corrected him.

"Front, bow, either way we're not allowed here."

Up and up we ran. At the top of the fourth flight of steps, a sudden smell of smoked herring hit us.

"Crew's kitchen!" shouted Omar. "This way!"

"Galley," I panted, running along the corridor behind him. "On a ship you say galley, not kitchen."

"Shut up," puffed Omar.

We sprinted past the sailors' cabins and galley, then burst through an unmarked door into the fresh, salty air. This well deck was a third-class area and it was crowded with third-class passengers playing different kinds of games: ring toss, marbles, Dutch skipping and arm-wrestling. Shouting and laughter mingled with the thrum of the ship's engines and the roar of the sea against its prow.

Omar and I split up. He joined a group of boys playing marbles, whilst I leaned over a railing and pretended to gaze out to sea. Out of the corner of my eye I saw our pursuer emerge blinking into the light. He scanned the deck for a minute or two, but soon gave up and went back inside.

I sat down on a hatch cover and promised myself never to enter a cargo hold again.

# CHAPTER

A man with a flat cap and a red moustache strolled past me playing the elbow pipes. He was playing an old Irish tune called 'Erin's Lament', and it reminded me of the afternoon we first boarded the *Titanic* at Queenstown. He had played 'Erin's Lament' that day, too. I remember thinking that it was a strange, sorrowful sort of tune for the maiden voyage of such a wonderful ship.

Everything about the Queenstown launch was still fresh in my memory. The cart ride from Kilkenny, the crowds milling around the harbour, the seagulls wailing and squawking. Most of all I remembered my first sight of the *Titanic*, with its colossal hull, gleaming decks and enormous smoking funnels.

Mum, Ralph and I had boarded the ship along a gangplank right here on the foreward well deck. A medical officer had checked my head for lice and made me stick out my tongue to check for scarlet fever. At the same moment I stuck my tongue out, I saw a young girl watching me from the first-class deck up above. She must have thought I was sticking my tongue out at her, because she stuck out her tongue right back at me!

I had seen the girl again a few times after that. She often came to stand at the railing, her duffel coat drawn tight around her body and her auburn curls blowing in the wind. Whenever she stood there watching the third-class passengers enjoying themselves, she looked a little sad. I guessed she would rather be down here having fun with us than up there in first class with her posh family.

I looked up at the first-class deck. Sure enough, there she was again, gazing down at the well deck.

Except this time, she was hanging upside down, gripping the railing in the crook of her knees.

"Beryl!" cried a woman in a long fur coat, hurrying towards her. "Stop that! You'll fall and kill yourself!"

"I'm fine, Mama," the girl replied, scowling at her mother upside down.

"You won't be fine when your body is splattered all over the well deck. Besides, those poor people down there have enough problems in their lives without you falling on their heads."

Beryl sighed and flipped herself the right way up. As she did so, two tiny slips of paper fell out of her duffel coat pocket and fluttered down onto the pedestal of a cargo crane below.

"Mama!" cried Beryl. "My gym tickets fell down onto the well deck."

"Thank heaven that's the *only* thing that fell onto the well deck," snapped the woman. "Come along, I'm taking you inside."

"But Mama, the tickets. . ."

"Leave them! Your father paid a thousand pounds for our parlour suite. He won't refuse you a shilling to replace a couple of gym tickets."

As soon as Beryl and her mother were out of sight, I made my move. I leaped from the hatch cover onto a metal rail, and from there onto the pedestal of the cargo crane. I reached out and grabbed the tickets before the wind could blow them away.

"Get down from there!" a steward on the first-class deck shouted at me. "It's not safe!"

I scrambled back down onto the deck and looked at the tickets in my hand.

---

### GYMNASIUM ADMITTANCE

The bearer of this ticket is entitled to one hour in the *Titanic* gymnasium, including unlimited rides on the electric camel.

*Ladies*: 9 a.m.–noon
*Gentlemen*: 2 p.m.–6 p.m.
*Children*: (ages 6 to 16): 1 p.m.–3 p.m.

---

Omar hurried over to me. "What were you doing on the crane?" he asked. "I heard the steward shouting at you."

"Nothing much," I said. "Just fetching these."

"The first-class gym!" Omar peered over my shoulder and his eyes almost popped out of his head. "I don't believe it. An electric camel!"

"Keep your hair on," I said. "You know that third-class passengers aren't allowed to use the gym."

"Who will know we're third class?" cried Omar. "Do we have 'third class' written on our foreheads? Come on, Jimmy, it's an electric camel! If we don't do this, we will regret it for the rest of our lives!"

# CHAPTER

Lunch in the third-class dining room was rabbit pie with potatoes, green beans and gravy. While we were eating, Omar told me stories of real camel rides he had been on back home in Lebanon.

"When you're about to climb onto a camel," he said, "never look in its eyes. And never ever stand in front of it, unless you want the top of your head bitten off."

"Thanks for the tip," I said. "And what about electric camels?"

"I have never met an electric camel," he chuckled, "but there's a first time for everything."

I did not have a suit, so Omar lent me one of his. He even gave me a tie to wear. By one o'clock, we looked like a very fine pair indeed. The only problem was, neither of us knew where the gym was.

"I thought you'd been everywhere on this ship," I said.

"Everywhere except first class," Omar admitted. "You?"

"Same."

"Here's an idea," said Omar. 'We'll use the ladders from the well deck. They go all the way up to the first-class promenade deck."

"You mean the ladders that are blocked by chains and no entry signs?" I asked.

"Yes."

"The ones overlooked from the navigation bridge?"

"Yes."

"Way too risky," I said. "Come on, I've got a better idea."

I led the way along Scotland Road past the bakery and the stewards' cabins. On the left, just before the turbine room, was a dull grey door marked 'STRICTLY NO ENTRY'.

"Stewards' stairs," I said. "I've heard they lead straight up to the first-class pantry."

"Come on, then."

As soon as the coast was clear, we turned the handle and slipped through the door. I felt a thrill of excitement through my whole body as I walked up the forbidden stairs.

Lunch was being served in the first-class dining room so the pantry was buzzing with activity. Stewards hurried to and fro with bottles of champagne and dishes of oysters, salmon and asparagus.

A chef with his back to us stood at a table laden with pork, beef and lamb. He was busy sharpening an enormous knife.

Omar tapped him on the shoulder.

"Excuse me, my good fellow," he said in a very posh voice. "Is this the gymnasium?"

"No, sir, this is the pantry," said the chef. "The gymnasium is up on the boat deck. Take the Grand Staircase all the way to the top, sir."

"Thank you," said Omar.

Trying not to laugh, we walked into the first-class dining room. Finely dressed people sat in comfortable armchairs, sipping fine wine and eating delicious-looking food. Nobody even looked at us.

Omar nudged me and pointed to a broad-shouldered man in a dinner jacket. He was sitting by a port-side window drinking coffee with a young woman.

"Do you know who that is?" asked Omar. "That's John Jacob Astor. My dad showed me a magazine article about him. He's one of the richest men in the whole world."

At the other end of the dining room, a steward opened a big oak door for us. We went through into a plush lounge with thick carpets, crystal chandeliers and – I'm not exaggerating – the most mind-boggling sight I had ever seen in my life.

# CHAPTER

Stretching before us was a beautiful staircase. I had seen pictures of the Grand Staircase on the *Titanic*, but as I walked up those stairs with Omar, I felt like I was in a dream. We passed priceless paintings, angels made of bronze and a fine clock set among carved wooden figures.

"It's like a stairway to heaven," Omar murmured.

Up on the boat deck, the first door we came to was marked 'Gymnasium'.

"Come in, come in!" said a handsome man, dressed

all in white. "I'm Mr McCawley. You've got your tickets there? Marvellous! Welcome to the gym. What do you want to go on first?"

"The electric camel," we said in unison.

"Of course." Mr McCawley twirled his moustache. "That's what they all say."

The electric camel had pride of place in the centre of the room. It was made of smooth polished mahogany with a leather saddle and a long graceful 'neck' of turned wood. It was mounted on a well-oiled metal pedastal, on which it rocked slowly to and fro to simulate the motion of a dromedary.

We took turns to ride the electric camel, increasing the speed each time. On the maximum setting the camel lurched wildly back and forth and we laughed ourselves silly as we clung on for dear life.

There was plenty of other equipment, too, of course. While I was on the camel, Omar tried the rowing machine and the parallel bars. While Omar was on the camel, I used the punchbag and the wall bars.

I was just about to begin my fourth ride on the camel when Beryl walked in. She recognized us immediately.

"Hello," she said brightly. "How did you two get in here?"

"Keep your voice down," I hissed.

"Did you use those tickets I dropped?"

"Maybe."

Beryl hopped onto the camel, turned the dial to a gentler setting and started to ride. "What are your names?" she asked.

"I'm Jimmy, and this is Omar."

"Is this your first visit to the upper decks?"

"Yes," I said. "It's fantastic. What's it like living in first class all the time?"

"Our parlour suite is gorgeous," said Beryl, "and the meals are wonderful, of course. But there aren't many children in first class. And I do miss my little Wilbur Wigglebottom."

"Who's that, your boyfriend?" I laughed.

"No!" She scowled at me. "My cocker spaniel. Mama won't let him in the suite, so he's down in the kennels, poor thing." Beryl got off the electric camel and started bashing the punchbag with her fists.

"Good punching," I said. "Remind me never to get in a fight with you."

She bashed the punchbag even harder. "You two should obey the rules and stay in third class," she said. "It's not fair that you get to roam around all the best first-class areas when I haven't even set foot in third class."

"What's stopping you?" said Omar. "You could come to one of our midnight parties."

Beryl stared at him. "Your parents let you go to *midnight parties*?"

"Sure," said Omar.

"My mam doesn't let me," I said, "but when she's asleep I put a decoy in my bed and sneak out. Maybe you should try that."

Beryl giggled. "Yes, maybe I should."

At that moment, the gym steward came up to us with a notebook.

"I'm taking a register," he said. "I need your names and cabin numbers."

"Beryl Balfour," said Beryl. "Cabin eleven."

"Mario Conti," said Omar. "Cabin twelve."

"Timothy... er... Turnip," I stuttered. "Cabin thirteen."

"Cabin thirteen?" Mr McCawley looked up sharply. "Are you sure about that, Master Turnip?"

"Positive," I said.

"That's odd," said Mr McCawley, "because there is no cabin thirteen on this ship. The number thirteen is considered unlucky."

"Oh," I said, sweating.

"And for you today it is definitely unlucky." The gym steward scowled and reached for my collar.

I dodged back out of the way.

"Here goes," groaned Omar. "More running."

# CHAPTER

When I went to bed that night, my legs ached. We had been chased by a sailor in the morning and a gym instructor in the afternoon, and somehow we had managed to outrun both of them.

"What are you grinning about, Jimmy?" said Ralph, leaning down from the top bunk.

"Nothing," I said.

"I've hardly seen you all day. Where have you been?"

"Oh, here and there," I said.

I closed my eyes and pictured the Grand Staircase with its plush carpet and gleaming curved banister. I remembered the sunlight pouring in through the glass dome above us, and the chandeliers that scattered the light into thousands of tiny rainbows.

As soon as Mam and Ralph were asleep, I arranged the decoy in my bed and crept out into the corridor. Omar was waiting for me at the end of Scotland Road.

"Good evening, Master Turnip," Omar said. "Ready for another adventure?"

"Sure," I said. "There's an American band playing in third class tonight. It's a new style of music called 'ragtime'."

"I've got a better idea," said Omar. "Let's go back up to first class and see what's going on there."

"How can we? We're not even wearing our suits."

"We can sit outside, Jimmy, on top of the glass dome above the Grand Staircase. We'll be able to see all the rich and famous people from there. We'll be like spies."

"I don't know," I said. "I've got a bad feeling about it."

"What if I told you that I've found a secret way of getting to the boat deck completely unseen?"

"Really? How?"

Omar grinned. "Tell me, Jimmy, how does this ship keep moving forward in the water?"

"Big engines down in its belly, powered by red hot furnaces."

"And for those furnaces to keep burning, what do they need?"

"Coal."

"What else?"

"Air?"

"Exactly." Omar grinned and gave me a thumbs up sign.

As soon as I realized what Omar's plan was, I shook my head. "No way. I'm not crawling up another air vent, especially not one filled with boiling hot air."

Omar sighed. "I'm not talking about the vent where the hot air goes out, Jimmy. I'm talking about the intake vent where the cool air comes in. It runs through all eight decks and it has rungs inside that we can climb. Come with me, Jimmy. I'll show you. You know you want to."

He was right. I did want to. "All right, you gombeen," I said. "I'll come."

"What is a gombeen?" asked Omar.

"Someone who is always doing crazy things." We headed downstairs to F Deck, then through the laundry room and into the drying room. Sheets and pillowcases from the first-class cabins hung all around. We climbed behind the hot-water pipes, opened a wooden hatch and crawled through into the intake vent.

# CHAPTER

# 10

The vent was warm but not hot. It echoed with the whirring of fans and the voices of furnace workers far below.

Slowly, carefully, we climbed the metal rungs. It was pitch black all around us and the rungs under my fingers felt slippery.

"Hey, Jimmy!" called Omar, climbing up below me. "Would you rather be a gombeen or a plonker?"

"I'd rather you shut up and let me concentrate on climbing."

At last we came out into the open air. We found ourselves on the roof of the boat deck next to the second funnel. It was cold up there, the kind of biting cold that gets inside your bones and makes your teeth chatter in your head.

Omar hopped across a low rail onto a glass dome. I followed him, and there below us was the Grand Staircase we had seen that afternoon. At the top of the stairs stood a group of gentlemen wearing dinner jackets and ladies in elegant ball gowns. The light from the chandeliers sparkled off their wine glasses and jewellerypearly white teeth.

They were watching a singer performing in the lounge below. She wore a long white dress and a feather boa, and she was prancing among the chairs singing a daft song about the moon.

*I'm such a silly when the moon comes out;*
*I never seem to know what I'm about;*
*Skipping, hopping, never never stopping,*
*I can't keep still, although I try.*

Omar wiggled his shoulders in time to the music. "I'm such a silly when the moon comes out," he crooned and I burst out laughing.

Just then, a door on the boat deck opened. I clapped my hand across Omar's mouth to stop him singing as two gentlemen came into the open, smoking cigars and talking in loud voices.

The taller of the two men I recognized as John Jacob Astor. He had a kind face and an American accent.

"Mr Futrelle, I love your detective books," he said. "*The Problem of Cell 13* was so exciting, I read it twice!"

The other man was short and hunched. "You are very kind, Mr Astor," he said, wiping the fog off his eyeglasses and lighting a cigar.

I was so close to the two men that I could have reached down and bopped them on their heads.

I didn't bop them, of course, but what I did do was almost as bad. I coughed.

It wasn't my fault. The smoke from their cigars caught in my throat and made me do it.

The men spun round and saw us perched on the glass dome. They stared, amazed.

"Zounds!" cried the famous writer. "What are you two doing up there?"

We did not stay to explain. We scrambled up the glass dome, slithered down the starboard side and sprinted along the boat deck towards the navigation bridge.

I was heading for the ladder at the bow when suddenly Omar grabbed me and pulled me behind a big wooden lifeboat.

Just in time, too. The door of the navigation bridge opened and out came a man with a white beard and two medals on his uniform.

"It's Captain Smith," whispered Omar. "Quick, Jimmy. Hide!"

The cover of the lifeboat was made of thick white canvas. Omar lifted the edge of the canvas and gave me a leg up so that I could wriggle into the boat. He dived in after me and pulled the canvas tight.

"That was close," I whispered. "What do you think the captain would do to us if he found us on this deck?"

"He'd probably make us walk the plank," Omar replied.

I chuckled at that. "He's Captain Smith, not Bluebeard the pirate!"

We stayed in the lifeboat a long time. If we had wanted to, we probably could have slipped out and made a run for it, but the boat made a great den, and it was also the perfect place to spy on the officers in the navigation bridge.

There were four benches inside the boat and more seating space around the edge. Omar found an electric torch under his bench. He kept switching it on under his chin to make scary ghost faces.

As we spied on the ship's officers, we talked in whispers. We talked of our adventures aboard *Titanic* and we compared dreams about our new lives in America. I said I wanted to become a rich businessman like Mr Astor. Omar said he would like to write adventure stories for a living.

"I'm going to start with a story about our adventures on this ship," he said. "*Omar Betros and the Ship of Dreams.*"

"Hey," I said. "How come I'm not in it?"

"You'll be in the sequel," said Omar. "*Omar Betros and the Little Irish Beggarboy.*"

I laughed. "Yeah, well I've got one for you. *Omar Betros Gets a Slap in the Mouth.*"

I grabbed his collar and we started play wrestling, but we were suddenly interrupted by the clanging of a bell high above us.

Omar lifted up the canvas and we peered up at the mast, the rigging and the tops of the ship's enormous funnels.

"Look," I said, pointing. "There's someone moving in the crow's nest!"

"What is the crow's nest?" said Omar.

"It's that platform halfway up the mast. There's a lookout up there. He's the one ringing the bell."

As the clanging continued, the lookout started to yell at the top of his voice.

"Iceberg!" he shouted. "Iceberg, right ahead!"

# CHAPTER

An officer at the navigation bridge picked up a phone and listened. His mouth dropped open. He slammed the phone down and yelled, "Full astern!" His voice was so loud, we could hear him even through the thick glass windows of the navigation bridge.

"He looks rattled," said Omar. "What does full astern mean?"

"It means, reverse the engines," I said. "He's trying to slow the ship down."

The officer yelled again. "Hard astarboard!"

"He's telling them to steer the rudder to the right," I said. "If they steer hard, we might not hit the iceberg."

I unhooked the canvas on the lifeboat and threw it aside. At first I saw only mist in front of the ship, but then I saw what looked at first like a big grey building, a mountain of ice as high as the ship's rail. And we were heading straight towards it.

"The ship isn't turning!" cried Omar. "Why is she not turning, Jimmy?"

"She's not a canoe, Omar. She's the *Titanic*. Turning takes time."

We stood up and watched, horrified. The bow of the ship swung slowly to the left and started to nose past the edge of the iceberg, but it wasn't enough. The iceberg struck the starboard rail near the navigation bridge, knocking me and Omar off our feet. We heard a dreadful crunching sound all the way along the hull of the ship. A clatter of ice shards rained down on the decks and the ship drifted on into open water.

"Phew, that was close," I said. "I thought we were goners."

"What are goners?"

"Dead people," I said. "But it's okay, we're past the iceberg now. Just scraped some paint off the rail, that's all."

We got to our feet. Far below us, our friends in third class were coming out onto the well deck to find out what was going on. When they saw ice all over the place they laughed and clapped.

"I thought only first class got ice for their drinks!" someone shouted.

"Ice fight!" cried another, chucking a ball of ice at a friend.

Brisk footsteps came towards us along the boat deck. There was no time to pull the canvas back into place, so we just ducked our heads down as Captain Smith strode past.

"What have we hit, Officer Murdoch?" demanded the captain, flinging open the door to the navigation bridge.

"Iceberg," said Officer Murdoch. "I ran the engines full astern but we were already too close."

Captain Smith went inside and closed the door. I could see him through the glass, barking orders to his men. Some of them hurried off to inspect the damage to the ship, others stayed on the bridge and busied themselves flicking switches and pulling levers.

"They seem really worried," said Omar. "If you ask me, that iceberg did more than scrape the paint, Jimmy."

Minutes passed. We stayed in the lifeboat, straining to hear the captain's orders on the navigation bridge. But it was no good. The glass was too thick.

Eventually, a man in a bowler hat arrived on deck and beckoned to Captain Smith. The captain came outside and they spoke together in low voices. They were standing just a few feet away from where Omar and I were hiding.

"You built this ship," said the captain. "You know her better than anybody. Tell me straight, Mr Andrews. Is the damage serious?"

# CHAPTER

# 12

"Very serious," said Mr Andrews. "The iceberg punched a hole in the starboard side of the ship. Water is coming in. The front five compartments are already flooded beneath the waterline."

"We have closed all the watertight doors," said the captain. "Do you think the ship can stay afloat?"

Mr Andrews paused for a long time before replying. "No," he said at last. "Two hours from now the *Titanic* will be at the bottom of the sea."

When we heard that, Omar and I both gasped out loud.

Captain Smith and Mr Andrews heard the sound. They peered over the side of the lifeboat and saw us crouching there.

"I don't know what you're doing in that boat, boys," said the captain, "but if you want to live, you'll stay exactly where you are." He turned to the ship builder. "Mr Andrews, we must tell the crew to prepare the lifeboats!"

Mr Andrews paled. "Captain, the *Titanic* has twenty lifeboats. That is only enough for half of the passengers."

"I know," said Captain Smith grimly.

As Captain Smith strode back to the bridge and took command, Omar turned and looked at me, his eyes as big as saucers.

"Did I hear him right, Jimmy? Did he just say that the *Titanic* is going to sink? And that there are only enough lifeboats for half of us?"

I couldn't speak. I could hardly believe my ears. This ship was a floating palace. It seemed so safe and solid. Could it really all end up at the bottom of the sea?

"We've got to get out of here," said Omar. "We need to warn our families."

We clambered out of the lifeboat, barged through the nearest door and ran down the Grand Staircase three steps at a time. There was no point staying hidden now. First class, third class, none of that stuff mattered any more. Getting to our families was all we cared about.

A group of gentlemen and ladies were coming up the stairs towards us. They sprang aside as we charged past, and one of the men reached out and grabbed me.

It was the American millionaire, Mr Astor.

"Take it easy, buddy," he said. "Why the hurry?"

"Sir, the ship is sinking," I gasped. "They're preparing the lifeboats. You need to go up to the boat deck straight away, sir."

The people around Mr Astor laughed and shook their heads, but he himself did not laugh. "Thank you," he said gravely, and let go of my arm.

We dashed through the first-class dining room and the pantry, and down the stewards' stairs to Scotland Road.

"We should split up," I told Omar. "You go to the bow and warn your family. I'll go to the stern and warn mine. Tell everyone you meet to find a lifejacket and go up on deck fast."

Omar nodded and dashed off along the corridor.

I ran towards the back of the ship, but Scotland Road was blocked by a metal barrier that hadn't been there before. It had no lock, no handle, nothing. I hit it with my fist but it was completely solid.

A steward came out into the corridor and saw me thumping the barrier. "You can't move it,' he said. 'It's a watertight door. Nothing to worry about, son. I'm sure it will open again soon."

"No, it won't," I told him. "The ship is sinking. We need to find a way through this door and wake everyone up."

The steward didn't believe me. Either that or he was too shocked to reply. He just stood there scratching his head and staring at the watertight door."

"What about D Deck?" I asked him. "Are there watertight doors up there as well?"

He shook his head. "Only on this deck and below."

I headed back up the stewards' stairs, turned left and ran through the first-class pantry, the galley and the second-class dining room. Nobody was here. The second-class passengers had already gone to bed.

There was a big brass bell attached to the dining room wall. I realized that this was the bell the head waiter rang at mealtimes, letting people know it was time to come and eat.

A bell was just what I needed right now, to raise the alarm in third class on my way to fetch my family. I flicked open my penknife and used it to undo the screws that held the bell bracket in place. As soon as the screws were loose, I pulled the whole thing off the wall.

"Hey, you!" A waiter hurried towards me, scowling darkly. "That bell is part of the furnishings. You're not supposed to—"

"The ship is sinking," I stammered. "Ask the officers if you don't believe me. You need to get everybody up onto the boat deck, fast."

Something about the expression on my face must have convinced the waiter that I was telling the truth.

"You in third class?" he asked.

"Yes."

"All right, you go down there, I'll go to second class."

We ran past the butcher shop and along the second-class corridor. The waiter started knocking on cabin doors, and I carried on running all the way to the staircase.

I took the steps three at a time, down, down, down into the belly of the ship, ringing the bell like crazy. As I reached G deck I stopped dead. The corridor ahead of me was an inch deep in murky water. It lapped gently from one side of the corridor to the other.

"Emergency!" I yelled. "Everybody up on deck! Bring your lifejackets!"

I took a deep breath and stepped down into the flooded corridor. Icy water seeped through the seams of my old shoes and enveloped my toes. I gasped at the shock of it.

Still ringing the bell, I splashed my way along the corridor as fast as I could. Sleepy passengers were wandering out of their cabins, awoken by my shouts. They rubbed their eyes and stared down in disbelief at the freezing water that swirled and eddied at their feet.

"Get up on deck!" I told them. "The ship is going down."

When I reached my cabin I yanked the door open and a gush of water flooded out over my feet.

"Mam! Ralph! Wake up!" I yelled, switching on the light.

# CHAPTER

# 13

Mam and Ralph opened their eyes. They blinked and screwed up their faces and Mam looked like she was just about to say something cross.

But then she saw the water on the floor of the cabin.

"Ralph, get out of bed!" she cried. "Jimmy, what's going on? Where's all this water coming from?"

"We hit an iceberg," I said, grabbing our lifejackets from under our beds. "The *Titanic* is sinking."

Even to my own ears it sounded impossible. I

could just as well have told them that aliens had landed on the boat deck or that our ship had been swallowed by a whale. The *Titanic* is sinking. Surely the most impossible four words I had ever spoken.

But the evidence was right there in front of us. The water was over our ankles now, and my toes were starting to feel numb.

"Get dressed," I told them. "It's bitter cold outside."

They threw on the nearest clothes they could find, and we helped each other put our lifejackets on. Gasping and shivering, we followed everyone else up the third-class staircase and out onto the well deck.

The well deck was dry and there was a crowd of passengers standing around. Some wore nightgowns, others were fully dressed. Many were dragging bags and suitcases with them. There was no panic yet, just shock and disbelief.

This was a third-class area, just like the well deck at the bow. A waist-high gate across the steps blocked us from reaching the second- and first-class decks.

"Everybody keep calm," said a steward on the

steps. "When I open this gate, please proceed to the boat deck and board the lifeboats."

From down here in the well deck, the boat deck seemed very far away. As I looked, I could see a lifeboat already being lowered towards the sea on thick ropes. It seemed to be only half full of passengers.

We stamped our feet and blew warm air onto our hands. "How long are they going to keep us down here?" muttered Ralph.

A distress rocket whizzed upwards from the navigation bridge and exploded in a shower of white stars. A small boy next to me began to cry.

I thought of Pa hundreds of miles away in Detroit. He had no idea of the trouble we were in.

"What are you waiting for?" Mam said to the steward on the steps. "There are women and children down here!"

"The women and children will be first, madam," he replied. "Just as soon as I receive my orders."

Nobody else protested. Half of the third-class passengers didn't speak English and had no idea what was going on. Those of us who did speak English were used to doing what we were told.

We waited in the well deck for what seemed a very long time, and the noise of steam escaping from the funnels above us sounded like a long drawn out scream.

Three more lifeboats were winched down into the water. Like the first one, these boats were only half full.

We watched the lifeboats row away into the darkness. "Mam," I said, "there's no use waiting here. We need to get up to the boat deck right now."

"This *is* the way to the boat deck," snapped Mam. "We'll be on our way just as soon as this dunderhead lets us through."

She raised her voice on the word 'dunderhead' and threw a bitter glance at the steward who blocked our path.

"Mam," I whispered. "I know another way."

Mam looked at me. "That's all well and good, Jimmy, but this ship is like a maze. We're safer waiting here."

Ralph put a hand on her arm. "You need to trust

him, Mam. I wasn't going to tell you this, but our Jimmy has been sneaking out of bed every night, exploring the ship. He knows these decks like the back of his hand. He'll get us to the lifeboat deck just fine, I promise."

Mam looked from me to Ralph and back to me again. "All right, Jimmy. Lead on. But just the three of us, mind. I won't be responsible for anyone getting lost."

We pushed our way through the crowd and back into the ship. I led Mam and Ralph up the third-class entrance stairs, through an unmarked door and along a series of second-class corridors.

"Jimmy, are you sure about this?" said Mam.

"He's sure," said Ralph.

Through the second-class dining room we went, then through the galley, the pantry and the first-class dining room.

By the time we reached the first-class lounge and the Grand Staircase, Mam and Ralph were staring around them in awe of the luxurious furnishings. In shock, too, that all this finery was about to sink to the bottom of the sea.

At last we came out onto the boat deck. The ship's

musicians stood in a huddle playing cheerful tunes on their cellos and violins, trying to keep everybody calm.

"Well done, Jimmy!" said Mam, ruffling my hair. "You've done us proud tonight."

The people milling about on deck were mainly first- and second-class passengers. We joined a large group of women and children waiting to be loaded into lifeboats. Some men wanted to go in the lifeboats with their wives, but the officers refused. "Women and children only," they kept repeating.

I saw Mr Astor standing next to one of the lifeboats. He was hugging a young woman and saying goodbye to her.

"But John, we've only been married eight months," the woman sobbed. "What is going to happen to you?"

The millionaire kissed his wife's forehead and helped her into the lifeboat. "Don't worry about me, my dear. I will take another boat."

At that moment, someone tapped me on the shoulder.

"Omar!" I shouted. "You made it!"

# CHAPTER

# 14

"Quick, come with me," Omar said. "Bring your family."

We followed Omar between two water tanks and came out on the starboard side of the ship. There were fewer people here and more chance of finding a lifeboat.

A dark-haired woman grabbed Omar's arm and spoke to him crossly in a language I didn't understand. She had three other children around her and was dragging a large suitcase. Omar's mother, I guessed.

"Where's your pa?" I asked Omar.

"He stayed behind on G deck," Omar replied. "Most Lebanese people don't speak English, only Arabic. My father is helping the stewards to direct them to the exits."

"He's a hero," I said.

Omar nodded and bit his lip. He looked as if he was about to cry.

"Try not to worry," I told him. "I'm sure your pa will get out all right."

An officer helped us into a lifeboat, first Omar's family and then us. A large woman in a fur coat was next in line. A man in a bowler hat was trying to coax her into the lifeboat, but she was refusing to go.

"I'm not leaving without our daughter!" she kept saying.

I thought I recognized her voice, but I could not remember where I had heard it before.

"I'll keep looking for her,' said the man in the bowler hat. "She must have woken up and gone for a walk on deck."

"If you're staying to look for her, then I'm staying too," said the woman.

The officer in charge of loading the boat stepped forward and took her gently by the hand. "Please, madam," he said. "Your daughter has almost certainly gone in one of the earlier boats. Children have absolute priority, you see. Captain's orders."

The woman let herself be bundled into the lifeboat. She sat down heavily and started sobbing into her hands.

Before our boat was even full, the sailors hooked ropes to each end and started lowering it down the side of the ship towards the water. I counted the decks as we descended. A Deck . . . B Deck . . . C Deck . . .

The woman in the fur coat took her hands away from her face and reached out towards the sinking ship.

"My darling girl!" she wailed. "Where are you?"

And then at last I recognized her.

It was Beryl's mother.

I remembered Beryl bashing the punchbag in the gym. I replayed our conversation in my mind.

*When my mam's asleep I put a decoy in my bed and sneak out. Maybe you should try that.*

*Yes, maybe I should.*

Immediately I knew where Beryl was. She had gone to find the third-class party in the common room. And it was *my fault*.

I leaned out of the lifeboat to look at the bow, where the third-class common room was. The water was already washing over the forecastle and down into the forward well deck, which was right above the common room. I looked back at Beryl's mother. Her face was streaked with tears.

I had to make it right. I stood up, climbed over Mam and Ralph and made my way to the back of the lifeboat.

"Jimmy!" cried Mam. "Where are you going?"

"Don't worry," I told her. "I'll get another lifeboat, I promise."

I bent my knees and jumped onto one of the winch ropes.

"Stop lowering!" cried someone up above.

"He's lost his mind," yelled another voice.

Perhaps they were right. Perhaps I had lost my mind. All I knew was, I had to find Beryl.

I gripped the rope tightly between my knees and began to climb, hand over hand. D deck, C deck, B deck. . .

"Jimmy!" Ralph shouted down below.

"You gombeen!" yelled Omar. "You plonker! Come back here."

B deck had private walkways for first-class passengers only. My winch rope hung at arm's length from the walkway railing. As soon as I was level with the walkway, I reached out, grabbed the railing, pulled myself over it and slipped through the nearest door into the sinking ship.

# CHAPTER

# 15

I found myself in a sitting room with comfortable leather armchairs and a fireplace. There was something strange about the floor, though. It seemed to be sloping down towards the bow.

As I stood there, a writing table slid across the room and crashed into the fireplace. There was no longer any doubt at all. This ship was sinking.

Mr Andrews had predicted that the ship would be on the bottom of the sea in two hours. And that was at least an hour ago. I staggered into the corridor and looked around me, trying to work out where I was. Through a glass panel to my right I glimpsed a fine clock set among wooden carvings. I was close to the Grand Staircase.

"Beryl!" I shouted, but there was no reply. Just the deafening hiss of steam escaping through the funnels somewhere above me.

A group of men ran up the staircase from below, their faces black with soot. I guessed they were furnace men escaping the flooded G deck.

"Hey, you!" yelled one of the men. "Come with us, quick! The ship is going down."

"I'm looking for a girl!" I replied. "Red hair, red shoes, blue duffel coat. Is she down there?"

"Does she have dead eyes and lungs full of water?" answered the furnace man. "Because that's the only sort of person down there right now. Look to yourself, laddie, and get out while you can."

I ran into the first-class elevator and shut the metal gates.

"Did you not hear me?" shouted the furnace man. "It's flooded down there."

But it was too late. I had already pressed the button

marked 'E' on the control panel. Down I went, my heart pounding in my chest.

When the elevator reached E deck, the sea came in. I had expected some water to seep in under the door, or up through the grate in the elevator floor, but no, it rushed in all at once, knocking me off my feet. It was freezing cold, this water – even colder than the river back in Kilkenny. I gasped for breath and lunged at the control panel, reaching for the button marked 'D'.

But the water got there first. There was a crackle and a tiny puff of smoke, and the next thing I knew, the control panel was completely under water. I fumbled around under the water, pressing any button I could find, but nothing I pressed had any effect at all.

The water was still rising. I could just about touch the floor with my toes. There was no time to lose.

I grabbed the metal gate, forced it open and swam out into the Scotland Road corridor. My ribcage tightened. My neck stiffened. My breath came in big jolting gasps.

*Cold. Cold. Cold.* That was all I could think at first.

And then another thought. *I've got to get out of this water.*

Scotland Road was a long corridor, and the third-class common room was all the way at the bow end. My body temperature was already dangerously low. Hypothermia could not be far off.

My pa and I used to swim together in the river in Kilkenny, and he warned me all about the danger of hypothermia. When you swim in freezing cold water, your blood gets shunted to your vital organs. Your muscles slow down, your arms and legs get weak and finally you stop moving altogether.

*Watch out for the cold, Jimmy*, Pa used to say. *It gets inside of you and fills you up.*

I grabbed a light fitting on the wall and hauled myself up out of the water. I hung there for a moment, dripping wet, trying to calm the rising panic in my mind.

My skin smarted and burned. My neck felt like it was clamped in a neck brace made of ice. My hands in front of my face were a lurid purple colour.

But that was not the worst of it. I realized with a pang of horror that I was not alone in this corridor. Others had fought their own battle with hypothermia, and lost. I could see them out of the corners of my eyes, dark shapes floating on the surface of the water. *Don't look at their faces*, I told myself.

So instead I looked up. And that was when I saw the pipes.

Running along the ceiling of Scotland Road were a tangle of electrical cables and four thick water pipes.

I reached up above my head and put my right hand on the pipe. Slowly and gradually, the numbness in my hand was replaced by a gentle warmth. I lifted both arms and hugged the pipe, then kicked up off the wall and gripped the pipe between my legs as well.

I hung there upside-down and let the warmth of the pipe pervade my body. Then I began to shuffle along it, hand over hand, edging my way towards the bow of the ship.

As the blood returned to my muscles, I was able to move faster along the pipe. I imagined I was a squirrel, shinning upside-down along a branch towards a stash of acorns. Or a spy on a secret mission, stealthily infiltrating the villain's lair. Anything to stop myself thinking about the ugly truth, and the hideous things that floated below me. *Not far now*, I told myself.

The closer I got to the bow of the ship, the higher the water level rose. I heard it beneath me, lapping at the walls of the corridor, then suddenly I felt its icy touch on the back of my head. *Come in*, it seemed to say. *The water's lovely.*

I craned my neck and looked around me. The ceiling of Scotland Road – and with it my pipe – sloped down into the water ahead of me and disappeared. The ship must be sinking bow first. My path was completely blocked.

"Beryl!" I yelled. "Can you hear me, Beryl?"

No reply. Just the continuous shriek of steam escaping from the funnels above.

I had to be close to the third-class common room. Ten yards, fifteen at most. And even if Beryl wasn't there, the common room was now my best chance of escape.

I undid the buckles on my lifejacket, relaxed my grip on the water pipe and let myself drop down into the icy sea. *Cold*, shrieked my brain. *Cold, cold, cold, cold, cold, cold.* I allowed myself three ragged breaths, then shrugged off my lifejacket, closed my eyes and dived down under the water.

*Ten yards*, I told myself as I dolphin-kicked my way along the corridor. *Fifteen at most.*

I opened my eyes for an instant and closed them again in pain as the freezing water burned my eye balls. But in that moment I had seen what I needed. A banister, a rail, a staircase leading upwards.

I had arrived at the third-class common room.

# CHAPTER

---

# 16

I half swam, half ran up the common room steps, then smashed up through the surface of the water and took a desperate, gasping breath of air. My legs were cramping. My fingers curled like claws. But I was alive.

The third-class common room was a mess. The tables and chairs had all slid down to the bow end of the room. Water was pouring in through open port holes and through the well-deck doors. An abandoned accordion floated past.

"Beryl!" I screamed.

She was not here. For all I knew, she could have found her way into a lifeboat already.

I waded to the well-deck doors, and pulled myself up the banister, fighting against the downward flow. Up on the well deck, the water lapped and swirled. I clung tightly to the pedestal of a cargo crane and edged my way up onto the crane itself, dragging myself clear of the freezing waters. I was no longer thinking about Beryl. I was simply trying to stay alive.

I was not the only person clinging to the cargo crane. There was a man above me. I recognized him as one of the Irish passengers from third class, a cheery chap from Limerick.

He did not look so cheery now. He clung there, teeth chattering loudly, not moving up or down.

"Hey, mister!" I called. "If we climb to the top of this crane, we can get to the upper decks and the lifeboats!"

He did not answer. He just stared down at me, his eyes wide with fear.

I grabbed his left boot and shook it gently. "Don't give up, mister. You'll be right as rain, you hear?"

The man took a deep breath and started to climb, dragging himself up slowly the crane towards the first-class deck.

I clambered up after him, patting his boot from time to time and talking all the while.

"Were you at the party, mister? Did you hear the Yanks? I heard they played ragtime tonight."

The man smiled weakly. "Never heard anything like it in all my life," he said.

"Mister, did you see a posh English girl called Beryl at the party? She came down from first class. Ten years old. Red hair, red shoes, blue duffel coat?"

The man nodded. "She's a nutter, that one."

"Why?" I said. "What did she do?"The man continued to heave himself slowly up the crane as he told the story:

"The Yanks were playing their ragtime songs and we were all dancing and carrying on, when suddenly the iceberg hit. At first it was a bit of a giggle, you know? People were having snowball fights and putting bits of ice in their drinks. Laughing fit to burst, we were. But then folks started coming up from below saying there was water in their cabins.

Well, that wiped the laughs off our faces, I can tell you. One of the stewards told us to get up on deck, but, your Beryl wasn't having any of it. She rushed off downstairs like a mad thing. *Down* the stairs, mind, where the water was pouring in. Screaming, she was, and shouting something about her bottom."

We were nearly at the top of the crane now. My fingers were numb with cold. My jaw ached. My ears and nose felt like they were frozen solid.

*Something about her bottom?*

I tried to think – tried to remember – but my mind was slow and foggy. Names and places floated in and out of my mind and I could not grab hold of any of them.

Suddenly, out of nowhere, it came to me. "Wilbur Wigglebottom!" I cried.

"Yes, that's it," said the man. "That's what she was on about."

"Wilbur Wigglebottom is her dog! She must have gone to rescue it."

I closed my eyes and tried to picture a map of the ship in my mind. I had been to the dog kennels on one of my exploring adventures. They were down on

F deck, if I remembered rightly, next to the potato-washing room.

My heart sank. Scotland Road was already flooded, so F deck was under water, too. If Beryl had indeed gone to the dog kennels, she would have certainly drowned there.

*Dead eyes and lungs full of water . . . that's the only sort of person down there right now.*

# CHAPTER

# 17

The man from Limerick reached the top of the luggage crane and hung there, hugging it tight. He was only a short way from the railing of the first-class promenade deck, the rail where Beryl had been standing the very first time I saw her.

"Mister!" I shouted. "You've got to jump now! Pull yourself onto the top of the crane and jump across to the promenade deck."

The man whimpered and clung on even tighter.

"Come on, mister!" I yelled. "You are supposed to

be the brave one out of the two of us! For crying out loud, mister, I'm twelve years old! Don't look back on tonight and be ashamed!"

That did it. The man clenched his jaw, snorted loudly through his nose and heaved himself up on top of the crane.

"Well done, mister!" I cried. "Now jump!"

The man half jumped, half fell towards the first-class deck. He hit the railing hard and flopped over it to safety.

I was just about to follow suit when the ship lurched suddenly to port side. A rigging rope snapped and my luggage crane rotated on its pedestal. There was nothing I could do except hold on tight and be swung out over the well-deck rail.

I clung there for dear life, with nothing but the icy ocean below me. "Mister, help!" I screamed. "Throw me a rope or something."

But he had already disappeared up a ladder onto the boat deck. Getting into a lifeboat was the only thing he cared about right now.

Hanging there above the Atlantic Ocean, shivering like mad, I had a good view of the *Titanic*. Electric lights blazed on every deck, and at the stern of the ship two huge bronze propellors poked up above the waterline.

I looked again. Yes, those were definitely the propellors. They should have been deep under the water, but here they were in full view. *Bizarre*, I thought. *From A deck all the way down to G deck, the stern of the ship is dry.*

I readjusted my grip on the crane and forced my foggy mind to count the portholes from the stern of the ship to the middle.

Counting. Calculating. Mapping.

And then it struck me.

*The kennels are right on the waterline. Beryl may still be alive!*

# CHAPTER

# 18

As I hung there, hugging the the top of the luggage crane, the front-most funnel of the ship broke off at its base and crashed down into the water below me. It caused a massive wave which rolled the ship slightly to port side – and swung my baggage crane swung back to its middle position.

Now was my chance. I heaved myself up until I was crouching on top of the crane, then flung myself over the rail onto the first-class deck.

*Made it!*

I lay there shivering on the ice-strewn deck. A lifeboat was being lowered down the side of the ship from the deck above. It passed close by me, and a woman in a feathered hat yelled at me to board the boat.

With all my heart I wanted to board that lifeboat, but the thought of Beryl's mother stopped me. Instead, I dragged myself to my feet and stumbled once again into the sinking ship.

The first-class corridor had bronze lamps on the walls and thick red carpet on the floor. It stretched up towards the stern as far as I could see, sloping upwards at such a crazy angle that I could no longer run without falling over. I crouched down and started crawling on all fours instead, bounding uphill on my knuckles and tiptoes like a baboon.

The corridor led to a posh Parisian café on the starboard side of the ship. Not so posh now, of course. Chairs lay all over the floor, surrounded by fallen pot plants and smashed china. I crawled among the wreckage to the second-class stairway that led down into the belly of the ship. The steps sloped dangerously away from me, so I slid down the banisters instead, yelling as I went. On another day, it would have been fun.

I tumbled down into a corridor on F Deck, near the engine room. Ahead of me a set of doors stood open and a dimly lit corridor sloped down into murky water.

"Beryl!" I yelled.

No reply.

The invading sea lapped to and fro, edging closer and closer towards me. Although the stern of the ship was doing better than the bow, it would all go the same way, right to the bottom of the Atlantic Ocean.

Four engineers staggered past carrying a massive metal pipe. They were so exhausted they did not even look at me. They just waded down into the water and splashed their way along the corridor with their heavy load.

I gritted my teeth and followed them. The ceiling lights flickered eerily and I kept hearing mysterious clanks and crashes, some of them close by.

The water was rising. At first it only came up to my ankles, but soon it was up to my knees. I waded as fast as I could past the engineers' cabins and the engine room, and at last I arrived at the kennel room. The door was open, the light was on and a cacophony of barking came from within.

"Beryl!" I shouted.

"Jimmy!"

Along the far wall of the kennel room, twelve cages were arranged in two rows of six. In the upper cages a bulldog and three terriers were barking their heads off. In the lower cages, which were already flooded, two collies and a spaniel were paddling furiously to stay afloat. Beryl stood in front of the spaniel's cage, trying to pick the lock with a hairpin.

"Beryl, the lifeboats are leaving. We need to get out of here!"

"Not without Wilbur," she said tearfully.

"Who's got the key to his cage?"

"The purser," she sobbed. "I tried his office but he wasn't there."

I pulled out my penknife and waded over to her. "Let me try."

I chose a small thin blade and wedged it as far into the lock as it would go. Then I took Beryl's hairpin, slid it in alongside the knife and wiggled it gently from side to side.

"Hurry up, Jimmy," said Beryl. "The water is nearly up to the top of the cage."

My fingers were numb and clumsy, and try as I might, the lock would not open. Wilbur pawed the bars of his cage, yelping in fear.

"Howdy!" boomed a voice behind us.

We turned and saw a tall man, wearing a dinner jacket and bow tie, wading into the kennel room. He was pointing a gun right at me.

# CHAPTER

# 19

"Mr Astor," I stuttered. "What are you doing here?"

"Same as you," he said. "I guess great minds really do think alike. Stand aside, kiddo, I'm gonna blow that lock to kingdom come."

Beryl and I jumped out of the way and covered our ears. BANG! The lock flew apart and Wilbur's cage door burst open.

"Wilbur!" cried Beryl, as her precious dog swam out into her arms. "I thought I'd lost you."

"Let's go!" cried Mr Astor. "Come with me, quickly now."

"No," said Beryl. "Look at all these dogs. They'll drown if we leave them."

"And *you'll* drown if you don't," snapped Mr Astor. "Come on, girl. Leave them."

Beryl shook her head and burst into tears again.

Mr Astor's features softened. He bent down and took Beryl's face gently between his hands.

"Look at me," he said.

Beryl turned her tear-stained face to look up at the millionaire.

"You and me, we're going to do a deal," said Mr Astor quietly. "If you and your friend leave now, I promise you I will stay here and free every last one of these precious dogs."

She nodded and he nodded back, and I grabbed Beryl's hand and we left. There were so many things I wanted to say to Mr Astor at that moment, and there wasn't time to say any of them.

Beryl and I waded out of the room and along the corridor, holding hands tightly and taking turns to be the strong one. When Beryl stumbled, I pulled her up.

When I stumbled, she pulled me up. The shots from the American's revolver echoed down the corridor as we ran towards the stairs.

Suddenly Beryl stopped. "Do you hear that?" she said. "Not the gun shots. The other sound."

I listened. There was a grating sound above us. It was getting louder and closer, as if something heavy was scraping down the port side of the ship.

"Lifeboat!" said Beryl. She waded to the nearest porthole, pressed her nose to it and squinted upwards. "It's going to come down right past us! Come on, Jimmy, help me get this porthole open."

We unfastened the porthole clips, and yanked it open. A moment later the lifeboat was alongside us, and we came face to face with a tearful, terrified woman wearing a thick, woolen scarf.

"Tell the sailors to stop lowering!" I shouted.

"Certainly not!" she snapped. "This boat is already full, can't you see?"

We weren't taking no for an answer. Beryl took off her duffel coat, wrapped Wilbur in it and handed him to me. I held the dog tight and crouched down so that Beryl could stand on my back. She launched herself headfirst through the porthole, wriggled her hips to squeeze through the narrow gap, and fell down into the lifeboat on the other side. The winch ropes creaked and strained.

"I said, there's no room, you silly girl!" cried the woman in the scarf. "You're going to swamp the boat and kill us all! Is that what you want?"

The other passengers said nothing. Packed tightly together, they crouched on their wooden benches and stared straight ahead, shivering and terrified, as the boat descended.

I reached through the porthole and threw Wilbur Wigglebottom to Beryl.

"Stop it!" shrieked the woman. "I had to say goodbye to my husband up there, and you're loading a *dog*? Are you completely witless?"

I grabbed the rim of the porthole and heaved myself up out of the freezing water. My head was poking through the porthole and I could see the lifeboat right below me. It had almost reached the water.

"Come on, Jimmy!" shouted Beryl. "You can do it!"

I wriggled and struggled, kicking my legs like mad to inch myself forward through the hole.

"Thank heavens!" cried the woman in the scarf. "His shoulders are too wide! Go up on the boat deck, young man, and wait your turn like everybody else! Though I'm pretty sure that this is the last lifeboat."

She was right, my shoulders simply would not fit through the narrow porthole. I watched helplessly as a crew member on the lifeboat unhooked the winch ropes and signalled to the sailors up above.

"Jimmy!" screamed Beryl. "Jimmy!"

The lifeboat drifted away from the side of the ship. Two people picked up an oar each and began to row away with long, quick strokes.

*I'm pretty sure this is the last lifeboat.* That was what the woman had said.

Half in and half out of the porthole, stuck fast by my shoulders, I watched *Titanic*'s last lifeboat row away into the night.

It was Beryl's fault, of course. Her and that stupid dog of hers. And the lookout's fault for not seeing the iceberg sooner. And Pa's fault for going to Detroit without us and making us travel on this stupid ship.

And God's fault for giving me wide shoulders.

I cried like a baby, I don't mind telling you, my tears running off the end of my nose and into the ocean below.

# CHAPTER

# 20

At last I managed to wriggle down out of the porthole, back into the flooded corridor. The water was rising even more quickly now. I half waded, half swam to the second-class stairs, and dragged myself up the banisters.

I realized that I was no longer shivering, and I remembered with a jolt something Pa once told me as we swam together in Kilkenny.

*Shivering helps to keep you alive, Jimmy. If ever you're so cold that you stop shivering, you'll stop living, too, soon enough.*

*What should I do, Pa?* I gasped as I stumbled up the stairs towards the upper decks. And I must have been going mad because I heard his answer in my head as clear as day. *Find some dry clothes and a lifejacket, Jimmy.*

That's what I heard. *Dry clothes and a lifejacket.* Bonkers.

Arriving on B deck, I slid down through the wreckage of the Parisian café and ran straight into one of the first-class cabins.

I looked quickly under the beds that had slipped to the bow end of the room, and I found a lifejacket under the third. Then I opened the wardrobe, which had toppled over onto its side. It was full of men's jumpers, socks and trousers.

All of the clothes were too big for me, but I didn't care. I tore off my freezing wet clothes and put on the dry ones. I completed my outfit with a long winter coat, a dry pair of boots and on my head two pairs of thermal underpants. I must have looked a right gombeen, but I didn't care a jot.

When I finally made my way up to the boat deck, it was a very different place to the one I had left. When

I was last up there with Mam and Ralph there were dozens of people milling around, but very few of them were panicking. Now there were hundreds – literally hundreds – of people on deck, and it was absolute chaos.

I recognized some as people we had waited with in the aft well deck of the ship. The red-haired man with the elbow pipes. An Irish woman with small children. Lots of Italians, shouting and carrying on. The stewards had let them come up on deck at last – far too late to save a single one of them.

The musicians were no longer playing. Instead of cheery violin and cello music there was only the hiss of steam from above and some mysterious clanks and bangs from down below.

And all around me, weeping.

And screaming.

And praying.

I held on to a metal ring near one of the three remaining funnels. From there I could see both the port and starboard sides of the boat deck. Along both sides, the lifeboat winches stood empty. That woman in Beryl's boat was right. All of the lifeboats were gone.

I had promised Mam that I would get another lifeboat, and now I had gone back on my word. I was going to go down with the ship

The bow of the ship nosed downwards into the icy water, so people were trying to drag themselves up the sloping deck towards the stern. I saw a mother pulling herself up with one hand and cradling her baby in the other. I saw a priest clinging to a luggage hatch, reaching down with his free hand to help others get on too. I saw stewards, waiters and furnace men diving into the water and trying to swim out to the lifeboats. Strangest of all, through the back window of the gym, I saw a man in a top hat riding the electric camel, with a huge smile on his face.

And then I saw something else. At the bow of the ship there were two lifeboats yet to be launched.

# CHAPTER

---

# 21

The last two lifeboats on the *Titanic* were invisible to almost everyone on the boat deck because they were stowed up on the roof of the officers' quarters They looked strange, these boats. Their bases were solid enough, but the sides were bare wooden frames. Skeleton boats.

Some sailors down at the bow climbed up onto the roof of the officers' quarters and began to lower the skeleton lifeboats towards the boat deck. I noticed then that each lifeboat had a roll of canvas around the edge of the hull, ready to be stretched up over the wooden frame. Once the sides were lifted into position, these boats would be as safe and seaworthy as any other lifeboat.

The young mother stood next to me, clutching her baby in one arm and holding on with the other. I nudged her and pointed at the lifeboats.

"Look there," I said. "Two extra boats!"

We ran and slid and rolled our way down the sloping deck towards the precious boats.

It was clear to everybody that the *Titanic* had only minutes left. The bow plunged down another few feet and the sea gushed right up to the level of the navigation bridge. An officer coming out of the wheelhouse was washed right off the ship. He didn't even get the chance to scream. He just disappeared.

As soon as the skeleton boats touched down on the boat deck, a team of officers attached them to the winches on the rail. "All aboard!" cried one.

I ran to the boat on the starboard side and was about to clamber in when someone crashed into me from behind and sent me sprawling on the deck. Dozens of people had spotted this one last chance of survival, and they were clustering around the boats like ants around two sugar cubes. I staggered to my feet and tried to get into the other boat, but the people were crushed together so tightly it was impossible to get through.

There was no way I was getting a seat in either of these boats, even though I'd seen them first. It was not fair.

But that was just it, of course. None of this was fair.

"That's enough!" the commanding officer cried. "Stand back! The collapsible boats are full!"

Once again the *Titanic*'s bow lurched downwards into the sea. The sudden swell of water lifted the collapsible boats off the deck and pulled them forward. The port side lifeboat drifted free, but the one on our side was still attached to the winches.

"Cut the ropes!" yelled a suited gentleman on board the lifeboat. "Cut the ropes, quick, or we're going to be dragged under!"

I whipped my penknife out of my pocket and threw it to the gentleman, who sliced through a rope with one quick motion. A steward did the same at the other end, freeing the lifeboat. It drifted away from the ship, leaving the rest of us on the *Titanic*'s flooding deck.

"Raise the sides!" shouted the commanding officer.

The people in the boats grabbed the rolls of canvas and started to stretch them up over the wooden frames. But as they did so, there was a sudden explosion at the base of the *Titanic*'s nearest smokestack. As if in slow motion, the whole enormous funnel toppled over and smashed into the water on the port side of the ship. A massive wave flooded over us and threw us all into the sea.

My lifejacket pulled me up out of the water, and I bobbed there on the surface, gasping for breath. All around me men, women and children kicked and screamed as the funnel disappeared without a trace.

One of the collapsible lifeboats was floating upside-down on the port side of the ship and the other one – the one I had helped to free – was drifting away on the starboard side, half full of water. The occupants of both boats were in the water.

I started swimming towards the flooded boat on the starboard side of the ship. In spite of the chaos around me, I felt strangely calm. I pretended to myself that I was swimming with my pa in the Kilkenny river and that the terrified screams around me were screams of excitement from Ralph and the other children. I imagined Mam calling to me "Come out now, Jimmy!" and me replying "Just one more minute, Mam!"

The cold saltwater stung my eyes and burned my throat, but I concentrated on my front-crawl technique, slicing through the icy water with the edges of my hands and breathing regularly like I'd been taught.

*Just one more minute, Mam.*

My clothes and shoes felt heavy on my body but my cork-filled lifejacket stopped me from being pulled under, and after a few more strokes, I found myself at the collapsible boat.

Gasping and shivering, I wriggled between the wooden slats and into the bottom of the lifeboat.

# CHAPTER

# 22

The last thirty seconds of the *Titanic* was terrible to watch. As the stern rose higher and higher into the air, dozens of people dived off into the sea. Dozens more slid down the deck, bouncing off rails and hatches as they went. I heard four massive explosions and then all the lights on board the ship flickered and went out.

With the bow so low and the stern so high, the pressure on the middle of the ship was too great. With a deafening crack, the *Titanic* broke clean in two. The front half of the ship disappeared beneath the sea and the back half crashed down onto the water, knocking yet more people off its deck.

The back half of the ship did not last long. It tilted to one side, tipped up on end and entered the water vertically like the tailfin of a diving whale.

The screams. The screams. I will never forget the screams as long as I live.

In the minutes that followed, sixteen people joined me on the flooded lifeboat: twelve men, one woman and three children. We sat along the rim of the boat and stared in horror at the patch of dark water where the ship of dreams had disappeared. We could hear it under the water, imploding and disintegrating as it went deeper and deeper.

I remember the floating wreckage around me: a deckchair here, a suitcase there, a couple of restaurant menus. I even thought I saw a crate marked 'dragon's blood' floating by, but maybe I imagined it.

I didn't imagine the people, though. They were all around us, gasping and splashing and dying.

The worst deaths were the ones that happened in our lifeboat. We managed at last to raise the canvas sides but there was so much water in the boat and not enough room for everyone to keep dry. The grown-ups decided they should take it in turns to kneel in the freezing water. Over the next hour, three of them died right there in front of us. They stopped shivering, went very still and slipped silently beneath the water.

You know what I remember most about that night, apart from all the terrible stuff? The stars! We never used to see many stars in Kilkenny, what with all the fog and streetlights, but that night afloat on the Atlantic, the sky was full of them: Orion, the Seven Sisters, the Big Dipper, the lot.

Thoughts tumbled over each other in my mind. What time was it in Kilkenny? Was it morning yet? What time was it in Detroit? Had Pa gone to bed yet? Was he asleep under these same stars? Was he dreaming? Was he calm and happy in his dreams, or tormented by distant screams and shadows?

Many of the survivors in the lifeboat were weeping for those they had lost or left behind. There was this man in a bowler hat sobbing like crazy, and he suddenly leaned over the side of the boat and called "Beryl!" at the top of his voice. Turned out, he was

Beryl's father. He had stayed on the *Titanic* until the very last minute, searching in vain for his daughter.

"Sir, she's alive," I told him. "She got on a lifeboat with Wilbur Wigglebottom. I saw her with my own eyes."

The man made a strange sound, something between a laugh and a sob, and he hugged me so hard I thought we were both going to fall overboard.

I could not help wondering what kind of sound Pa would make when he heard of my survival.

Or my death.

# CHAPTER

# 23

After an hour or two, we drifted alongside a proper wooden lifeboat, which was only half-full. We begged them to let us climb across onto their boat, and eventually they agreed. The new lifeboat was better than the collapsible one. It was dry. That was the main thing.

I sat cross-legged in the bottom of the boat and stared ahead of me. Someone gave me a biscuit from the ration locker, and I ate it in a hundred tiny bites, wondering how long it would be before the lifeboat rations ran out. Hours? Days?

In one terrible night our vast floating city had shrunk to a tiny skiff adrift in the Atlantic. Did anyone even know of the fate which had befallen the *Titanic*?

Was anyone coming to rescue us?

Anyone?

Ever?

Sometime later, I was woken by a loud fog horn. I sat up and saw a bright light shining straight at us. I blinked and shielded my eyes.

Beryl's father was cheering and waving and jumping up and down. "A ship!" he cried. "We're saved!"

I was so tired and cold, I was only half aware of what happened after that. I think the ship sent out small boats to rescue us. I remember being told to sit in a basket and being hauled up onto the deck. And I remember getting out of the basket and being attacked by Mam. She hugged me, kissed me, shouted at me a bit and then hugged me again. Ralph hugged me, too. I was too tired to stop him.

"We thought we'd lost you," said Ralph. "You went

a bit crazy there, Jimmy, running back into the ship like that."

"I didn't go crazy," I said. "I'll tell you the whole story later."

"Hear that, Mam?" said Ralph with a wink. "Our Jimmy says he didn't go crazy. I'd believe him, I would, if he wasn't wearing pants on his head."

At nine o'clock in the morning the last *Titanic* survivor was brought aboard and the rescue ship set sail for New York. Mam said the name of the ship was *Carpathia*. Even the name sounded welcoming and kind.

All of us survivors were taken below decks and we were each given a blanket and a mug of hot milk with sugar. My hands were so cold and numb, I could not even hold the mug at first. And then when I finally managed to pick it up, my lips were too numb to drink it properly. The milk kept dribbling down my chin.

Ralph grinned at me. "Do you want a spoon for that?" he said.

An officer from the rescue ship was walking up and down with a clipboard, asking for everybody's name and address so that he could make a list of survivors.

"Omar Betros," I heard one boy say.

I jumped up and ran over to him. Like me, he was wrapped in a blanket and clutching a mug.

"Omar!" I cried. "Good to see you!"

"Hello, Jimmy." Omar's voice was flat and tired. "I'm happy you're alive."

"Me, too! Any news of your father yet?"

Omar shook his head. "Somebody gave me this. They found it floating in the water."

He put down his mug and took something out from under his blanket. It was a musical instrument shaped like a teardrop, with delicate swirls of mother-of-pearl set into the polished wooden surface. I recognized it immediately as the oud that Omar's father had played at the third-class party.

"Doesn't mean he's dead," I gulped. "Doesn't mean anything at all."

"Yes, it does," whispered Omar. He blinked twice, hunched forwards and started sobbing.

I've never seen anyone cry so hard. At first I just stood there staring at him, not knowing what to do, and then I knelt on the floor in front of him and hugged him while he wept.

So many memories of the *Titanic*. There are some good memories, of course. No one can take those away from us. Roof dancing. Dragon blood. Electric camel. Polished banisters. Bronze angels. Gleaming chandeliers.

Terrible memories, too. Memories that will haunt me at night for as long as I live. Rending metal. Falling funnels. Screams in the darkness.

But when I think of the *Titanic*, there is one image that comes to my mind more often than any other. My friend Omar wrapped in a blanket, clutching his father's Lebanese lute, crying his eyes out.

I survived the sinking of the *Titanic*, but 1,522 people did not. May every single one of them rest in peace.

# HISTORICAL NOTE:

# THE SINKING OF THE *TITANIC*

**THE SHIP**

When it was built, the *Titanic* was the largest ship in the world. She was longer than three football fields and taller than a seventeen-storey building.

Her maiden voyage (first journey) started from Southampton on 10 April 1912. She picked up extra passengers in Cherbourg, France and Queenstown, Ireland, then headed for New York, USA. At 11.40 p.m. on 14 April she struck an iceberg. See page 128 for a timeline of the last hours of the *Titanic*.

## THE PEOPLE

Neither Jimmy nor Omar are based on real people, but I did read one exciting true story of a boy who survived the sinking of the *Titanic*. Jack Thayer was seventeen at the time of the disaster. He jumped into the water as the ship sank and somehow managed to swim out to a lifeboat.

### Omar's father

There were ninety-three Lebanese passengers on board the *Titanic*. Omar's father is based on Al-Amïr Farïs Shihäb, a talented Lebanese musician who was travelling to America hoping to make his fortune there. He played the oud, which is a Lebanese string instrument similar to a lute. He often played it to entertain passengers aboard the *Titanic*. When the ship began to sink, he directed many women and children to the exits, then played his oud to calm those who remained on board. He went down with the ship.

### Captain Edward Smith

Captain Edward Smith was the captain of the *Titanic*, responsible for the safe navigation of the ship and for managing all crew members. Captain Smith captained many ships during his career. He was once asked what he would do if one of his ships sank. He replied, "I would go to the bottom with the ship". He was last seen standing in the wheelhouse on the bridge of the *Titanic* as it was engulfed by the sea.

*Thomas Andrews*

Thomas Andrews was the shipbuilder who designed the *Titanic*. After the ship hit the iceberg, Mr Andrews informed the captain of the damage and told him that the *Titanic* would definitely sink. He also told the captain that there were not enough lifeboats on the ship. (Lifeboats were kept to a minimum in order to cut costs and to keep the decks from being too crowded.) Thomas Andrews went down with the ship.

*Jacques Futrelle*

Jacques Futrelle was an author who wrote many detective stories. His most famous stories were about a detective who was so clever that he was nicknamed 'The Thinking Machine'. He was last seen standing on the deck of the *Titanic* smoking a cigar with John Jacob Astor.

*John Jacob Astor*
John Jacob Astor was an American millionaire and a man of many talents. He was a businessman, an inventor and even a science-fiction author. His wife, Madeleine, survived the sinking of the *Titanic*, but Mr Astor perished. There are many stories of his heroic actions during the sinking of the ship. He is said to have helped raise the alarm in third class, and also to have freed the dogs from their cages.

## PLACES

The layout of the *Titanic* was exactly as described in this book. All of Jimmy and Omar's secret and not-so-secret passageways through the ship would have been possible. You can study deck plans of the *Titanic* at https://www.encyclopedia-titanica.org/titanic-deckplans/

*The gym*
The gym on the boat deck of the *Titanic* was

supervised by Thomas McCawley and it did indeed have an electric camel.

### The dog kennels
The kennels were down on F deck. They housed twelve dogs, three of which survived the sinking. The ones that survived were not in the kennels at the time of the sinking. They were spending the night in their owners' cabins, and were taken aboard lifeboats with their owners.

### The cargo holds
There were several cargo holds in the *Titanic*. The cargo on the maiden voyage included a Renault towncar, a marmalade machine and several crates of dragon's blood. However, Jimmy and Omar would have been disappointed to learn that the dragon's blood on board had nothing to do with dragons, but was a bright red plant sap used in nail varnish.

# THE LAST HOURS

*Sunday, 14 April 1912*

**11.39 p.m.** The lookout, Frederick Fleet, spots an iceberg in the water ahead of the *Titanic*.

**11.40 p.m.** The *Titanic* hits the iceberg on the starboard side of her bow. Water floods in through the hole in her hull.

*Monday, 15 April 1912*

**12.00 a.m.** Thomas Andrews tells Captain Smith that the *Titanic* will sink in less than two hours.

**12.05 a.m.** Captain Smith tells his crew to prepare the lifeboats and orders the radio operators to call for help.

**12.20 a.m.** The lifeboats start being loaded with women and children.

**12.25 a.m.** Fifty-eight miles away, the *Carpathia* picks up the distress call and starts sailing towards the *Titanic*.

**12.45 a.m.** The first lifeboat is launched less than half full.

**1.15 a.m.** The water is up to the name plate on the bow

of the *Titanic*. As the bow goes down, the stern is beginning to rise.

**2.05 a.m.** The last lifeboat is launched, but more than 1,500 people remain on the ship.

**2.10 a.m.** The stern is now far up out of the sea.

**2.17 a.m.** Captain Smith announces, "Every man for himself."

**2.18 a.m.** The lights go out.

**2.19 a.m.** The Titanic breaks in half. The bow half sinks.

**2.20 a.m.** The stern half fills with water and sinks.

**4.10 a.m.** The *Carpathia* picks up the first of *Titanic's* lifeboats.

**8.30 a.m.** The *Carpathia* picks up the last of *Titanic's* lifeboats.

**9.00 p.m.** The *Carpathia* arrives in New York carrying 705 *Titanic* survivors. 1,522 victims have died at sea.

## THE ENQUIRY

After the disaster there was a public enquiry. Survivors were interviewed to find out why the disaster happened. Among the conclusions of the enquiry were the following:

- The *Titanic* was lost because she was going too fast in a region of ice.
- None of the crew of the *Titanic* were at fault.
- In future, ships should carry enough lifeboats for all of the passengers.

# GLOSSARY

## NAUTICAL TERMS

**boat deck** the topmost deck of the ship, where the lifeboats are

**bow** the front of a ship

**crow's nest** a platform half way up the mast, where the lookout stands

**forecastle** the foremost exposed (outside) deck of the ship

**galley** kitchen

**navigation bridge** the area at the front of the boat deck from where the ship is commanded.

**port** the left side of the ship

**purser** an officer in charge of cargo and other valuables

**starboard** the right side of the ship

**stern** the back of a ship

**well decks** the lowest exposed decks of the ship

**wheelhouse** a room within the navigation bridge which contains the ship's wheel

## MUSICAL INSTRUMENTS

**elbow pipes** Irish bagpipes, played with the elbow

**oud** a Lebanese instrument with eleven strings, similar to a lute

**IF YOU ENJOYED**

# SURVIVOR
## TITANIC

**READ ON FOR A TASTE OF**

# SURVIVOR
## ESCAPE FROM POMPEII

# PROLOGUE

---

## 24 AUGUST AD 79
## POMPEII

I hurried to the square in Pompeii and saw eight priests, standing in a circle, offering loud prayers to the god Vulcan. Next to them was a pile of wooden crates, each with squawking chickens inside. Standing by the crates was a soldier with a knife in his hand. A crowd had gathered round the priests.

Then I saw my father. He was climbing up on a plinth. A statue had fallen off the plinth and lay broken beside it.

To my horror, he began to shout at the priests and the people.

"People of Pompeii, listen to me! This earthquake is nothing to do with Vulcan. Vulcan does not exist!" As the people turned away from the priests and looked towards my father, horrified by his words, he pointed towards the mountain Vesuvius.

"This earthquake is caused by the fires raging under Vesuvius. There is nothing you, or the priests, can do about it. Vesuvius will explode. And when it does it will shower this city with hot ash. Rivers of fire will pour down from the mountain. You will all die unless you leave now and get to higher ground away from the mountain. Flee!"

There were loud shouts of anger from the crowd, as they began throwing rocks at my father and shouting: "Silence him! It is his fault! He insulted Vulcan!"

The rocks hit my father and he fell backwards onto the cobbles. I ran to help him up, as others also rushed towards him, some arming themselves with wooden sticks.

My father scrambled to his feet, grabbed me by the hand and dragged me into a side street. He was bleeding from a gash in his head where a stone had hit him.

"We have to make people see the truth, Marcus!" he panted. "We have to save them!"

"No!" I shouted at him. And now I felt tears stinging my eyes. "They're right! This earthquake is all your fault. You have insulted Vulcan! I hate you! I hate you!"

And with that, I ran away from him as fast as I could.

Hot flakes rained down. The earth shook. Buildings cracked and fell. People cried out in fear and ran.

# CHAPTER

1

Our small two-wheeled cart trundled along the winding country road, pulled by our old horse, Pallas. We were on our way to Pompeii. It's a journey that my father, Lucius, and I do every year. We travel from our small cottage in the country, twenty miles outside Pompeii, to celebrate the Festival of Augustus with my father's brother and his family: my Uncle Castus, Aunt Drusilla and their six-year-old twins, Fabius and Julia.

There are lots of festivals throughout the year,

mostly in praise of the gods to keep them happy with us. The gods are all-powerful and there are hundreds of them, each one ruling a different part of life. There is Neptune, who controls the sea; Mars, the god of war; Venus, the goddess of love; Vulcan, the god of fire and volcanoes. Vulcan lives in a huge cave, deep beneath the earth, where he hammers at his forge making gates to control the fires that rage underground. Over them all is Jupiter, king of all the gods. We don't attend many of the festivals to celebrate the gods. My father says he doesn't believe in the gods. He says things happen because of nature, not because gods cause them to happen. I wish he wouldn't talk this way, but he does. Sometimes I think he says things like this just to annoy people. Other times I think he does it because he is mad. The priests have warned him not to say such terrible things – they believe that the gods will take revenge on him.

Uncle Castus says that my father became crazy when my mother was killed in an earthquake ten years ago. I was just two years old at the time. I can't remember much about my mother. I remember the warm smell of her when she cuddled me, but that is about all.

After the earthquake my father was left to bring me up on his own.

My mother's death made him so angry he began to speak out against the gods, saying they must hate humans to kill us like that. Then he started saying that there were no such things as gods. He said everything that happened was a natural thing: earthquakes, rain, volcanoes and storms – they were nothing to do with the gods. He said if we learned to understand nature we could stop these dreadful things happening.

At first people laughed at him, but when he carried on saying things like that the priests said he was mad and dangerous and would be locked up if he didn't shut up.

But my father didn't shut up. And they didn't lock him up. So he carried on saying the same mad things.

The trouble was other children didn't want to be friends with me, because of my father.

When he wasn't saying mad things about the gods, my father worked as a land engineer. It started because of his obsession with earthquakes and volcanoes – trying to find out how and why they happened. He studied how different plants grew better in different soils, how water drained faster from some places than it did from others, and everything else to do with land. The result was that farmers and landowners hired him to get the best crops from their fields.

And they were glad to pay him, until inevitably the subject of the gods would come up. They would ask him which gods they should sacrifice to in order to get the best harvest, or to make their lambs and goats grow faster. When they did this, my father would start his rant about how there were no such things as the gods. When he did that, the farmers would tell him they no longer wanted him on their land – they believed if he stayed, the gods would punish them.

That was why we never had much money. Every time he started a new job, it would go wrong. By the time I was eight my father had the reputation of a madman, and no one would hire him. So we lived in our small house. My father fed us with fruit and vegetables he grew, and we both cut wood to keep the fires warm.

Now and then we'd travel to Pompeii to visit my uncle and his family, and stay the night with them before travelling back home. Or sometimes we'd go to Herculaneum, the next big town. I was always glad when we did this because it was fun to be in a busy town, with the markets and lots of people bustling around.

At this time of year we travelled to Pompeii twice: once for the festival of the harvest, celebrating the crops being gathered in, and again for today's festival celebrating Augustus, the first and greatest emperor of Rome. It was Augustus who created the Roman Empire, which rules the whole world.

Yesterday had been the Vulcanalia, when sacrifices and prayers were said for the god Vulcan. This is why I thought it was strange when I felt the ground begin to shake beneath me. There had been other signs on our journey that showed that Vulcan was unhappy: the sound of thunder from beneath the earth; smoke coming from the mountain, Vesuvius. Vesuvius was just two miles from where we were, and towered over the landscape. We often had small earthquakes and earth tremors, but these seemed stronger than usual.

Why was Vulcan so angry? Had yesterday's festival not been to his liking?

Pallas, our old horse, stopped suddenly while pulling our cart along the country road. He stood, trembling, his ears laid back in fear.

"Vulcan is angry," I said.

"There is no Vulcan, Marcus," said my father. "Haven't you listened to anything I've told you? This earthquake being is caused by the volcano, Vesuvius, not by a god.

"Shut up!" I shouted angrily at him. "The gods will strike you down for saying that!"

Suddenly there was a huge tremor and a crack appeared in the road ahead of us. Pallas let out a frightened neigh and reared back.

There was the sound of an explosion from Vesuvius. Huge rocks began to roll down the mountain, some of them heading straight for us. A massive boulder bounced from a field and hit our cart. My father and I were hurled out onto the road. I was just scrambling to my feet when I saw another huge boulder hurtling towards us.

CRASH!

My father and I just managed to dodge to one side, but the boulder smashed into the cart. I saw Pallas fall to the ground. As I ran towards him, I could see that our old horse was dead.

# CHAPTER

I was standing looking down at poor Pallas and thinking that this was Vulcan's revenge for what my father had said, when I heard my father call out, "Marcus, look at this!"

I turned and saw that he had run into a field. I ran after him, and saw that there were sheep lying on the ground.

"They're dead!" he shouted. This seemed to make him happy, which I thought was odd. But then, a lot of what my father did was odd.

"Smell that air, Marcus!"

I did. It stank. It was like the smell of bad eggs, but much worse. And it was hot.

"That's what killed these sheep. The smell is coming from holes where the ground has cracked open. It's coming from the fires under the ground. The fire from the volcano is spreading beneath the earth. It proves I'm right! We must hurry to Pompeii and warn the people!"

"Warn them about what?"

"That the volcano is building up to an eruption. If that happens, Pompeii will be in danger. Come on, Marcus! We have to hurry!"

"We can't go anywhere," I said. "The cart is broken and Pallas is dead!"

I looked again at our poor dead horse. I felt tears come to my eyes as I remembered all the happy times I'd spent with him: walking behind him as we ploughed our small field, and riding him as he trotted gently along.

"We can run! shouted my father. "We aren't far from Pompeii."

He started to run along the road towards the city.

I shook my head in disbelief. I couldn't understand how he could be so heartless about Pallas! But when my father got obsessed, he didn't pay attention to anything else; not to me, not to Pallas, not even to our home. I ran after him.

"No, father! Please stop saying these things!" I pleaded.

"But I'm right!" he said as we ran. "The bad smell shows that gases are being forced out from under the ground. It's caused by pressure from the volcano. With that sort of pressure building up, Vesuvius is going to explode. And when it does, all that fire will come out in rivers of hot rock. They will pour down on Pompeii. We have to warn the people that they must leave the city."

"No! Father, stop! Please just stop." I shouted. "This is happening because Vulcan is angry. The mountain is shaking because something must have gone wrong at the Vulcanalia yesterday. That's what the priests say, and they know about this sort of thing! Earthquakes happen all the time, but they don't mean that a volcano is going to blow up."

My father shook his head.

"This one is different. The priests are wrong. Prayers and sacrifices won't stop the mountain blowing up and killing everyone. Even if the people won't listen to me, we must get my brother and his family to safety."

He carried on running. As always, I felt angry at the way he embarrassed us by insisting he was right and everyone else was wrong. Why couldn't he just be normal? I was sure the priests would find a way to make Vulcan happy and Vesuvius would settle down.

But then I thought of the earthquake that had killed my mother, and so many others, ten years ago. If things did get worse, then we had to help my uncle and aunt and my two little cousins to safety.

I ran after my father, towards Pompeii.

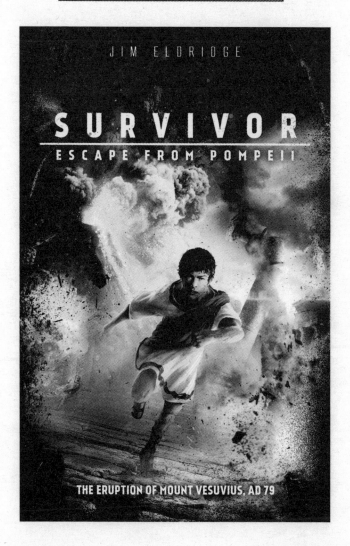